My Hair Is MAGIC!

To God's laughter and the blessings it brings.
Thank you for being both my inspiration and motivation.
Forever my loves, Nani and Lilah with an h.
— M. L. M.

To my Daughter, my joy, my heartbeat, Zoë!
— T. E.

Text copyright © 2020 M. L. Marroquin
Illustrations copyright © 2020 Tonya Engel

First published in 2020 by Page Street Kids
an imprint of
Page Street Publishing Co.
27 Congress Street, Suite 105
Salem, MA 01970
www.pagestreetpublishing.com

Distributed by Macmillan, sales in Canada by The Canadian Manda Group

20 21 22 23 24 CCO 5 4 3 2 1

ISBN-13: 978-1-62414-981-8
ISBN-10: 1-62414-981-2

CIP data for this book is available from the Library of Congress.

This book was typeset in Doodling.
The illustrations were done with printmaking, acrylic, collage, and oil.

Printed and bound in Shenzhen, Guangdong, China

Page Street Publishing uses only materials from suppliers who are committed to
responsible and sustainable forest management.

Page Street Publishing protects our planet by donating to nonprofits like The Trustees,
which focuses on local land conservation.

My Hair Is MAGIC!

M. L. Marroquin

illustrated by Tonya Engel

PAGE
STREET
KiDS

When people ask me,
"Why is your hair so BIG?"

I ask them,
"Why isn't yours?"

My hair is big,
my hair is beautiful.

Big like clouds,
SO beautiful it draws a crowd.

My hair is magical,
my hair is musical.

Tresses that enchant,
strands that entrance.

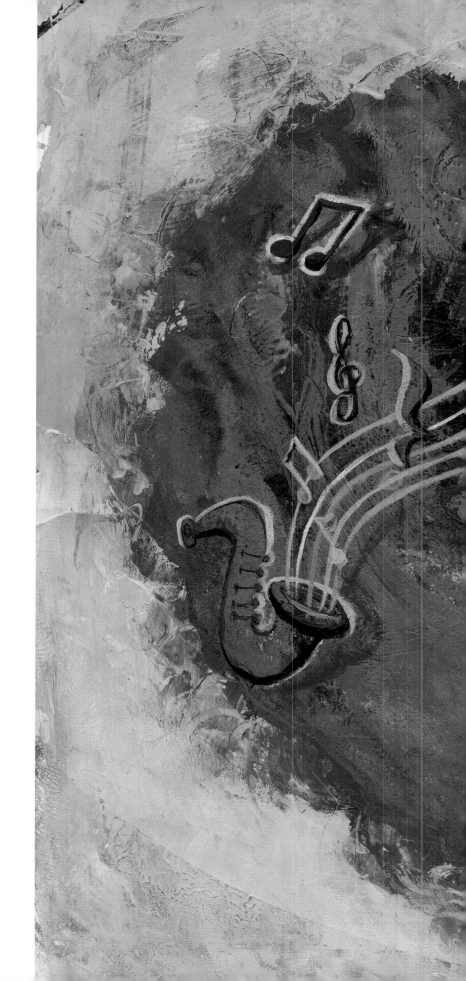

When people ask,
"Can I touch? Does it feel rough?"
Sometimes I say,
"Yes," and then, "That's enough!"

Sometimes I say,
"No! I need space!"
My hair needs room
to grow with grace.

My hair is gentle,
my hair is fierce.

Calm as a summer breeze,
powerful as ferocious bears.

My hair is soft,
my hair is brave.

Soft as fine sand,
fearless as surfers riding waves.

When people ask me,
"Don't you get hot under there?"

I smirk and respond,
"It's my protective layer."

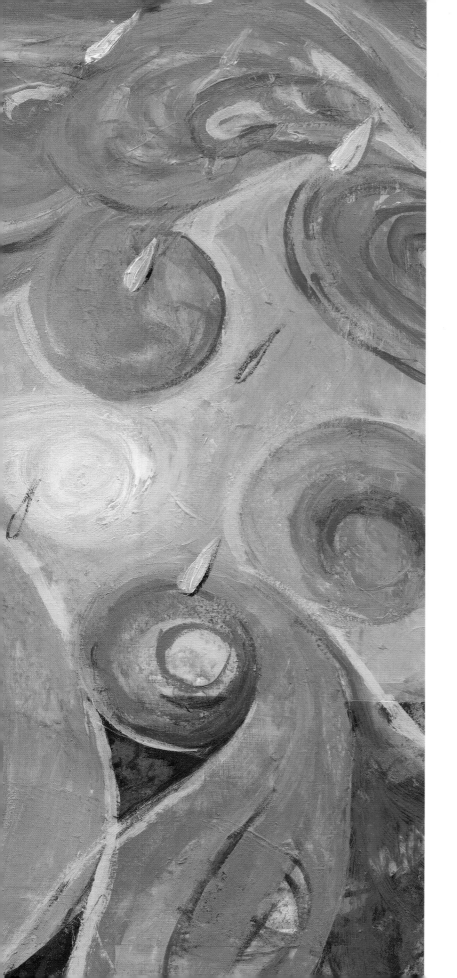

My hair is fire,
my hair is cool.

Hot as the desert sun,
cool as winter rain.

When people ask me,
"How do you comb all that hair?"

My mom answers,
"With tender love and care."

My hair is lush,
my hair is deep.

Rich as my ancestral roots,
deep as the Caribbean Sea.

People may wonder,
"Why isn't her hair straight?
Or in a ponytail
or waves?
What about twists,
or locks,
or gold beads in braids?"

My hair has flow,
my hair has soul.

Rhythmic as waterfalls,
warm as an embrace that consoles.

My hair has power,
my hair has spirit—
EVERY way I wear it.

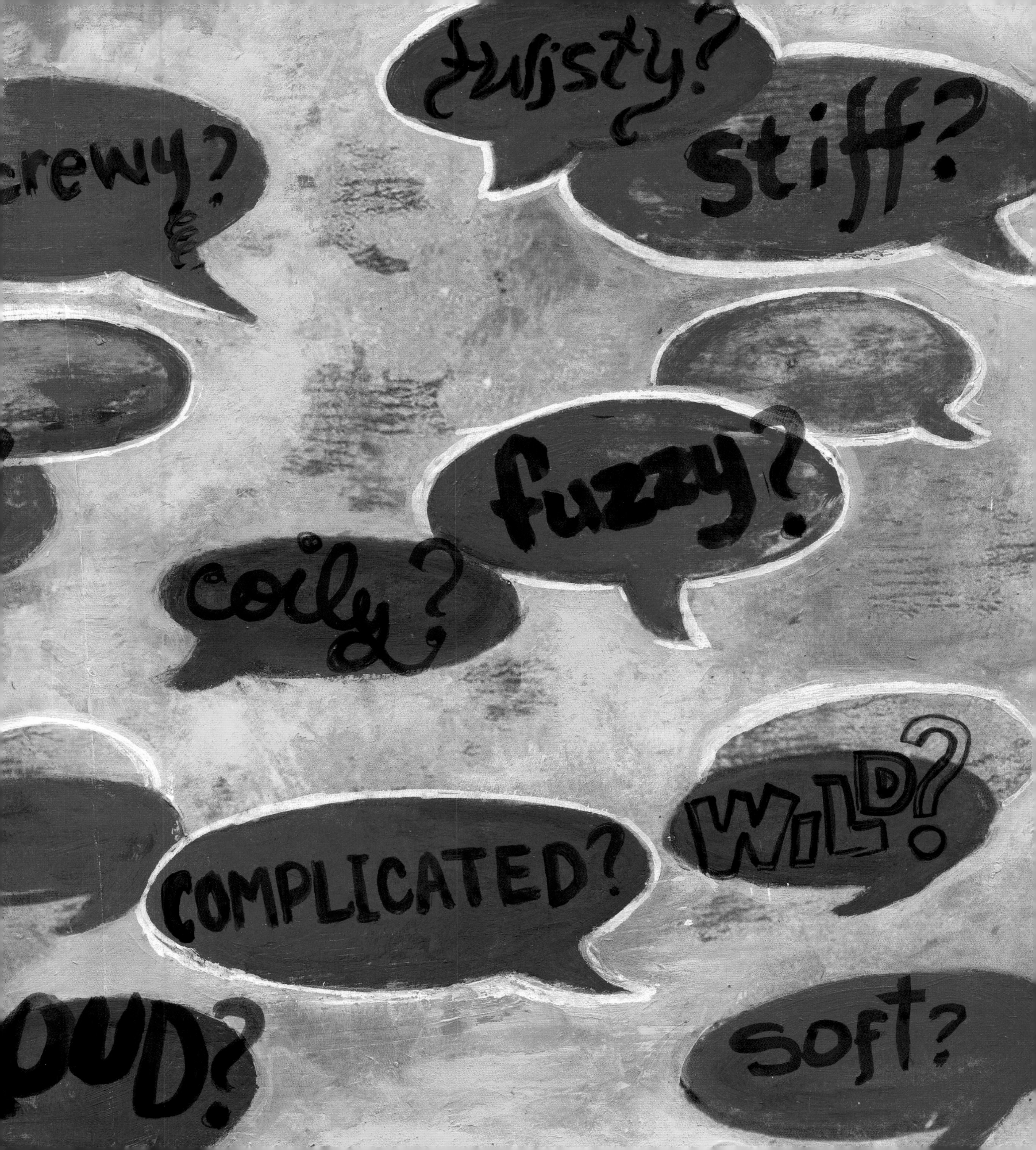
twisty?
stiff?
fuzzy?
coily?
WILD?
COMPLICATED?
soft?

I say,
"My hair is natural.
My hair is beautiful.
My hair is free. . . ."

My hair is ME!"